The Last Dreamers

James Barton

Contents

Prologue

In the hushed whispers of the elders, a time before the Bubbles is remembered, an era when ancestral spirits walked the land, their wisdom carried on the winds of memory. They speak of a distant age when traders from the land of the rising sun brought tales of the Baku, a dream-devouring beast that consumed nightmares.

But the Baku found a new home in the spirit world of Africa, merging with a once-benevolent ancestral guardian of dreams. Corrupted by a ravenous darkness, this spirit became uMdli wephupho - the one who eats dreams, leaving hollow shells of dreamers in its wake.

For centuries, the Dream Eater slumbered, its power held at bay by ancient rituals and unwavering faith. But as the world changed and the whispers of the ancestors faded beneath the relentless hum of modernity, the old ways were forgotten, and the seductive allure of manufactured escapes took hold.

The arrival of Dream Dust, a whispered promise of oblivion, awakened the Dream Eater, fueling its insatiable hunger. It seeped into the Reverie, the shared dreamscape, twisting its wonders into nightmares.

Now, the Dream Eater stalks the Reverie, growing stronger with each dream consumed. The ancestors' whispers are faint, their strength waning. In this liminal space where reality and dream intertwine, the fate of the dreamers hangs in the balance.

Only those who remember the old ways, who dare to confront the darkness within, can hope to stand against the Dream Eater. They must navigate the shifting topography of memory and desire, seeking the fragments of light that still flicker amidst the shadows.

For in the quiet spaces between heartbeats, entire universes are reimagined, and the transformative power of dreams can be reclaimed. The dreamers must become cartographers of their own souls, tracing the contours of their fears and hopes, to weave a new tapestry of reality from the threads of their own remembered light.

Chapter 1

Between one heartbeat and the next, where memory splits open like a ripe fruit, spilling dreams, Willa mapped the territories of other people's consciousness. Dreams crystallised on her tongue each one a landscape of possibility, a topography of desire and fear that burned sweet as sugar, sharp as grief. The Reverie stretched before her, a living atlas of the collective unconscious.

Tonight's dreamscape breathed beneath her feet, each grain of sand a mnemonic pulse, a synapse firing in the mind of a sleeping city. Buildings rose like liquid thought made manifest, their architecture defying not just physics but the very grammar of reality. They wept stardust and whispered in voices that tasted of childhood summers and lost alphabets.

She crafted bridges from the raw stuff of memory, spanning chasms between what was and what might have been. Rainbow-spun pathways solidified beneath her tread, each step leaving crystalline echoes that sang back to her in the frequency of forgotten lullabies. Here, in this liminal space, she was cartographer and creator both, mapping territories that existed only in the soft tissue between synapses.

The dreamscape cracked open, geometries spilling forth like broken egg yolks of impossible light. Towers woven from tomorrow's whispers stretched toward a sky painted in colours that existed only in the space between thoughts. A lion made of dawn-light and dusk-shadow prowled the rooftops, its mane flickering with the same fever that burned in Willa's blood when she walked the boundaries between consciousness and oblivion. Vines thick as ancestral stories wrapped around buildings that breathed like sleeping giants, their flowers opening to reveal eyes that had witnessed the birth of galaxies.

Her laughter scattered like quicksilver through the dream-thick air, transforming a castle built from yesterday's wishes into birds that wore sunset on their wings. They carried fragments of memories in their beaks, bright shards of moments that cut when they caught the light just so, each one a story waiting to be devoured or preserved.

Deep in the city's dreaming heart, where reality folded into itself like origami made of time, she encountered beings born from humanity's oldest narratives. Serpents with feathers made of prophecy and eyes that held tomorrow's secrets. Butterflies vast as hope itself, their wings cartographies of choices never made. Beside her padded a creature of starlight and shadow, ancient as ritual, new as morning, its form shifting between jackal and panther with each pulse of the dream-tide.

The creature's fur felt like midnight against her palm, its purr resonating with the same frequency as the ancestors' songs that usually guided her path. Understanding passed between them in the language of blood and stardust, a knowledge older than words, deeper than memory.

Here in the Reverie, she was more than the girl who lived where Cape Town's edges crumbled into myth. Here, she conducted symphonies of possibility, rewrote the laws of reality, danced on the knife-edge between memory and prophecy. Each dream she tasted added another layer to her internal map, another constellation in her private geography of consciousness.

But something soured in the dream's sweet air. Colours began to fade like old photographs left in the sun, while the sand beneath her feet whispered warnings in voices too faint to catch. The ancestors' songs stuttered into static, replaced by a dissonance that tasted of burnt sugar and lost time. A sweetness crept into the air, cloying as death.

The dream was changing. Reality was bleeding through its seams.

Consciousness slammed back like shattered glass beneath bare feet, each shard reflecting a different lie about waking. Willa's tiny apartment materialised around her, its shadows holding echoes of the Reverie's fading splendor. Outside, the Bubble mocked her with its sterile perfection, its manufactured dreams as hollow as dawn promises.

"Willlla?" Thabo's voice carried through the wall, thin as hope.

Her brother shuffled in, a geography of angles and shadows, his eyes holding something that made her heart stutter in its ancient rhythm. The sweet scent of Dream Dust clung to him like a shroud, and Willa felt reality crack along familiar fault lines.

"Just checking," he mumbled, but each syllable mapped territories of lies and chemical dreams, leading to places she feared to follow.

The truth hit her with the weight of falling stars: Thabo was using. Her brother was dissolving himself in false dreams, becoming a ghost while his body still breathed, each inhalation of Dream Dust erasing another piece of his internal landscape. The familiar sweetness of Dream Dust stirred memories Willa had buried in the deepest territories of her mind. Three years ago, she too had walked those chemical dreamscapes, each hit carving new neural pathways through her consciousness, until the boundary between reality and reverie became thin as smoke. The Dust had promised escape from the crushing weight of existence in the shadows of the Bubble, had whispered sweet lies about freedom and transcendence.

She remembered the way it felt: that first crystalline rush as synthetic dreams bloomed behind her eyes, reality fracturing into kaleidoscopes of pure possibility. How easy it had been to lose herself in those manufactured heavens, each dose rewriting the cartography of her desires until nothing else mattered. Not food. Not shelter. Not even Thabo, waiting at home with hunger in his eyes and questions she couldn't answer.

The withdrawal had been a geography of pain, muscle and bone and synapse all screaming for relief. She'd mapped new territories of suffering, chartered unknown continents of need. For weeks, her dreams had tasted of ash and endings, her consciousness a broken landscape of want and regret. The ancestors had been silent then, turning their backs on her chemical apostasy.

But she'd clawed her way back to reality, rebuilt herself one memory at a time, until she could walk the dream-paths again without that sweet poison singing in her veins. She'd promised h erself...promised Thabo...that she would never return to that particular wilderness.

Now, watching her brother disappear into the same devastating cartography, Willa felt the old hunger stir, a cartographer's itch to follow him into those forbidden territories. But she knew better now. Dream Dust didn't create new realities; it only consumed the ones that already existed, until nothing remained but the endless appetite for more.

Her fingers traced the old track marks on her arm, scars that read like braille beneath her fingertips, telling stories of loss and redemption. Each one a warning, a map of places she must never visit again. She could still taste it sometimes, in the depths of true dreams, that artificial sweetness that promised everything and delivered only hollow echoes.

A message flickered across her retinal display, its glyphs writhing like hungry things:

"Dream integrity compromised. Welcome to the Reverie."

Behind the words, something ancient and hungry watched through eyes that had never known light. The Dream Eater was waiting in territories unmapped, in the spaces between breaths, and it had already begun to feast on the cartography of souls.

Chapter 2

G rief is a landscape without mercy, a terrain so vast and unforgiving it threatens to consume everything.

In the soft interstices between memory and dream, landscapes breathe. Her memories were not linear passages, but living topographies trembling with unspoken histories, pulsing with the raw electricity of survival.

The day everything fractured began with a held breath. A pause between heartbeats. The silence crept in like rising water, first at the edges, then a flood that drowned every familiar sound. Not the gentle quiet of dawn, but the suffocating stillness that follows when the world stops turning, the suffocating quiet that follows catastrophic loss. This was the kind of silence that hollows out a home, that turns familiar spaces into mausoleums of memory. Willa was sixteen, and the word "orphan" felt like a brand, a mark of separation from the world of normalcy.

Her parents' absence had texture, rough as unsanded wood, cold as morning tiles against bare feet. Their absence leaked memories like slow-healing radiation, each remembrance carrying its own specific gravity: the sandalwood scent of her father's camera bag, the chalky residue of her mother's charcoal sketches still staining the desk's edge. In the corner of their small apartment, her father's photography equipment remained untouched, cameras with lenses that had once captured impossible moments now gathered dust, silent witnesses to a life interrupted. Her mother's botanical journals lay spread across the small desk, half-finished sketches of rare Cape flora frozen in time, the pages becoming brittle with each passing month.

Thabo was nine. Too young to understand the full magnitude of their loss, but old enough to feel the seismic shift in their universe.

In the quiet spaces between heartbeats, entire universes are reimagined.

The Anatomy of Addiction

Addiction is not a linear narrative. It is a living ecosystem, complex and interconnected. Each hit a negotiation with darkness, each moment a delicate dance between annihilation and transcendence.

The first time Willa touched Dream Dust, her hands shook, not with fear, not with anticipation, but with the raw voltage of desperation. This wasn't rebellion burning quick and hot; this was survival, cold and calculating. Each crystalline grain promised escape, but beneath that promise lurked a deeper truth: some doors, once opened, become mirrors instead of exits.

Grief is a landscape without mercy, a terrain so vast and unforgiving it threatens to consume everything. Social workers circled like vultures, their clipboards and sympathetic eyes promising to separate her from Thabo. The system was a machine that ground down the vulnerable, that saw two orphaned children as problems to be solved, not lives to be protected.

Dream Dust came as a whispered promise. A technology of escape. One touch, and the brutal edges of reality would soften, would transform into something bearable. Something beautiful.

Her first journey into the Reverie under Dream Dust's influence was not a descent, but an explosion of possibility. Colours that had no name in human perception. Sounds that existed beyond traditional understanding. A world where pain was just another malleable substance, something to be reshaped, transformed, dissolved.

She remembered selling her mother's silver locket. The pawnshop's fluorescent lights felt like accusation, like judgment. But the dust promised escape. Always, the dust promised escape.

Memories are not archives to be catalogued but living ecosystems.

Whispers of Contamination

The dreams began to change. Subtly at first.

Colours grew sharp, almost caustic. Landscapes that once flowed with impossible beauty now carried jagged edges. The creatures of the Reverie, those magnificent beings born from collective imagination...started to twist. Metamorphose.

Something was hunting in the dreamscape.

It began with small disruptions. A shadow at the periphery of perception. A frequency that didn't belong. Dreams that no longer felt like personal landscapes but like invaded territories. The beautiful, fluid world of the Reverie - that collective unconscious where imagination met raw possibility started showing signs of contamination.

Willa noticed how the dream creatures changed. The serpentine beings with emerald feathers now moved with a jerky, mechanical precision. The luminous butterflies left trails not of shimmering dust, but of something darker. Viscous. Almost mechanical.

The Hunting Grounds

In the Reverie, dreams were living entities. Malleable. Transformative. But something was consuming them. Not merely consuming harvesting. Extracting some fundamental essence that left behind hollow shells.

Melusi's investigation revealed fragments. Dream Dust production sites that appeared and disappeared like quantum anomalies. Manufacturing zones that existed in liminal spaces between regulated territories. Each site bore the same microscopic signature. A contamination. A frequency that didn't match human neurological patterns.

The supply chain was more than a simple drug network. In the spaces between transactions, something older stirred. The Dream Dust dealers spoke of profit margins and market territories, but their ledgers held a different truth: each sale marked in ink was really a coordinate on a map of hunger. Some customers reported hearing their dreams speak in voices that belonged to no human throat, while others swore the dust itself had begun to move against gravity, drawing patterns that resembled ancient glyphs in the air before dissolving.

Resonant Inheritance

Willa came to understand that her addiction had been more than personal weakness. It was a threshold. A doorway.

The Dream Eater required carriers. Conduits. Those whose neurological boundaries were already compromised. Those who had learned to move between worlds with fluid ease.

Her own journey through addiction had been a preparation. A training ground.

Some memories are keys. Some inheritances are portals.

The Gathering Darkness

As evening approached, the boundaries between past and present grew permeable. Willa felt the weight of her inherited knowledge, genetic, and experiential. A way of perceiving the world that existed between raw survival and something more profound.

The Dream Dust. The Reverie. The Dream Eater.

Interconnected systems. A living network that pulsed with its own dark intelligence.

And Thabo now stood at the threshold. Another potential carrier. Another doorway.

The light fades. Shadows lengthen. And in the quiet, the landscape of inherited darkness continues its eternal, subtle movement.

Welcome to the Reverie.

The Shadows Deepen

The whispers of "uMdli wephupho" - the one who eats dreams - carried ancestral memories that predated human understanding. Willa knew this now, not through scholarly knowledge, but through a visceral inheritance that pulsed beneath her skin like an ancient, forgotten language.

Her grandmother's stories echoed in the silence of their apartment. Tales of spirits that walked between worlds, of dream guardians corrupted by a hunger older than civilisation. The elders had warned of this moment, their voices lost in the technological cacophony of the modern world, dismissed as relics of a forgotten time.

The Dream Dust was more than a drug. It was a key. A portal.

A transmission.

Each night, the boundaries between her world and the Reverie grew more permeable. The dreamscape, once a sanctuary of impossible beauty, now resembled a battlefield. Contaminated. Mechanical. The serpentine beings with emerald feathers jerked, movements that spoke of something fundamental being extracted, harvested.

Thabo sensed it too.

His eyes, deep wells of inherited wisdom, held a sadness that transcended his nine years. He understood something profound about their inheritance - about the Dream Eater's patient, calculated hunger. The creature was not merely consuming it was transforming dreams. Reshaping the very fabric of collective consciousness.

Her survival would demand more than passive resistance. The first time she consciously wove a dream, reality stuttered like a skipped heartbeat. Colours separated into their component frequencies; time stretched like taffy pulled by invisible hands. Her fingers moved through spaces that existed between conventional dimensions, each gesture leaving trails of possibility that tasted like ozone and starlight. The nightmare threatening Thabo began to unravel, not dissolving but transforming, its sharp edges becoming soft as moth wings, its dark core splitting open to reveal veins of phosphorescent hope.

The elders' stories whispered back to her: some were chosen not just to witness, but to transform.

The traders from the distant land of the rising sun had brought more than stories. They had brought a seed. A possibility. The Baku myth had found fertile ground in African spiritual landscapes, merging with ancestral guardians in ways that defied linear understanding.

"We are carriers," Willa whispered to Thabo one night, her hand tracing the intricate patterns of their family's dream-map...a genealogy written in frequencies rather than blood.

The apartment walls seemed to breathe. Memories leaked like slow radiation. Her mother's botanical journals. Her father's impossible photographs. Each object a fragment of a larger, more complex narrative.

The Dream Eater's hunger was growing. Willa could feel its presence...a viscous darkness that existed between perception and reality. It was not hunting in any traditional sense. It was harvesting. Extracting some fundamental essence that left behind hollow architectural shells of consciousness.

Technology had prepared the ground. Dream Dust was merely the vector. The transmission mechanism for something older. Something hungrier.

Outside, the city continued its mechanical rhythm. Social workers. Bureaucratic systems. Clipboards filled with statistics that could never capture the true complexity of their existence. They saw two orphaned children. Willa saw portals. Thresholds.

Inheritance

At night, the dreams changed. Colours grew sharp. Almost caustic. The luminous butterflies left trails not of shimmering dust, but of something darker. Viscous. Mechanical. The Reverie was no longer a sanctuary but a hunting ground.

Thabo would watch her, his gaze both ancient and childlike. He began to understand that she was more than his sister. She was a key. A potential portal through which the Dream Eater might enter the world of the living.

The elders' warnings had been precise. The old ways were fading. The whispers of ancestors growing fainter with each technological pulse. But some inheritances could not be erased. Some blood memories ran deeper than forgetting.

Willa stood at the window, watching the city's lights blur into impossible geometries. The boundary between inside and outside, between dream and reality, had become meaningless.

In the drawer of her mother's desk, Willa discovered an old photograph. The photograph carried frequency, resonance, the kind of truth that vibrates in bone rather than brain. Her great-grandmother's eyes held geometries that didn't belong to standard mathematics, pupils like dark portals to older ways of knowing. When Willa touched the photo's surface, her fingertips registered textures that shouldn't exist in paper: patterns that moved like living things, warmth that pulsed with tidal rhythms, echoes of songs that existed before human voices learned to shape sound.

The Dream Eater was approaching. And they would be ready.

Chapter 3

Memory is not archive. Memory is landscape.

In the trembling interstices between perception and dream, Cape Town existed as a living organism, each street a nerve ending crackling with bioelectric potential, each boundary a permeable membrane exhaling unspoken histories. The city sprawled beneath a copper-tinted sky, its surfaces refracting sunlight through layers of environmental filtration, where reality folded and unfolded like origami landscapes of potential, the air sharp with the metallic bite of recycled dreams and ozone.

The Membrane's Geometry

The Bubble wasn't just another architectural marvel; it pulsated as a biotechnological ecosystem, its quantum-enhanced processors humming at frequencies that made teeth ache and dreams stutter. Its surface, a mesh of carbon nanofibers and synthetic neurons, filtered more than mere atmospheric pollutants – it curated human potential itself. The membrane's surface rippled with data streams, bioluminescent patterns flowing like digital rivers across its translucent skin.

Beyond the pristine barrier, earthbound rainbows shimmered where light caught the toxic particulates that the Bubble's filters rejected. These artificial auroras painted the lower city in shifting watercolours of pain and possibility. The air here carried layers of scent: ozone from malfunctioning filters, the sweet decay of synthetic fertilisers from vertical farms, and the sharp antiseptic tang of public sanitisation systems.

At the peripheral zones, where makeshift dwellings pressed against the Bubble's iridescent surface, human resilience birthed a new architectural language. Salvaged solar collectors gleamed like dragon scales, their surfaces etched with microscopic circuits still carrying fragments of corporate data. The panels harvested not just sunlight but electromagnetic whispers from above, each one a crystalline archive of discarded affluence. Every improvised structure defied scarcity; each repurposed component sang with the raw poetry of survival.

Willa and Thabo: Life Outside the Bubble

Their apartment clung to the city's weathered bones, where the recycled air tasted of rust and distant rain. Willa and Thabo's living space measured exactly twelve steps by nine, the walls sweating condensation from overworked atmospheric processors. The moisture carried whispers of chemical gardens, sweet and sharp against the tongue. Faded holophotos flickered weakly on beige walls, their power cells nearly depleted, images stuttering between past and present like fevered memories.

The kitchenette's sonic cleaner hummed off-key, its filtration system leaving traces of mineral residue that painted brown fractals across the steel sink's surface. Each morning, they scraped away yesterday's patterns only to find new ones blooming by nightfall, a calendar of decay written in rust and lime.

Willa traced her fingers along a wall's moisture-beaded surface, feeling the subsonic vibrations of the Bubble's environmental systems. "Sometimes I think these walls are drinking our memories as well as our moisture," she murmured, nostrils flaring at the copper-penny scent of recycled air.

Thabo sprawled on their transformable furniture unit, his eyes reflecting the iridescent afterglow of Dream Dust. Minute crystals still clung to his neural interface ports, refracting light in impossible geometries. "The space isn't what suffocates us," he replied, voice rough with synthetic stimulant residue. "It's their algorithmic indifference filtering down from above."

Life Inside the Bubble: A World Apart

Above them, the Bubble's interior unfolded in crystalline perfection. Smart-glass walls shifted opacity in response to thought patterns, while quantum-purified air carried subtle hints of alpine meadows and solar-distilled ocean. Residents glided through spaces where reality flexed like memory, their augmented nervous systems interfacing seamlessly with environmental controls that anticipated desires before consciousness could name them.

The air itself seemed to caress skin with molecular precision, each breath a carefully curated symphony of stimulation and calm. Light danced through programmable surfaces, creating environments that responded to emotional frequencies with architectural empathy.

A soirée bloomed in a penthouse bioengineered to evoke natural wonder. Programmable orchids released mood-enhancing spores, their petals shifting color in harmony with guests' emotional states. The engineered blooms filled the air with an otherworldly fragrance, something between jasmine and electric storms.

Antigravity platforms suspended crystalline decanters of molecularly-perfected wine, each vintage enhanced with nanoscale euphoriants that promised to unlock new territories of perception.

"The new Dream Dust formulation," a guest remarked, their prototype neural laces glowing soft gold at the temples, "it's not just creativity enhancement. They say it lets you taste the dreams of others."

Their companion laughed, irises cycling through designer chromatic patterns. "Careful with that hunger. Some dreams weren't meant for sharing." The words hung in the air like frost, a momentary crack in the perfect facade. Even here, in the heart of privilege, subtle acts of resistance bloomed. Some residents secretly disabled their emotional monitors, while others shared unfiltered memories through unauthorised neural bridges.

Beyond Official Narratives

The Bubble's algorithms sang their endless song of separation, quantum processors calculating worth and worthlessness in endless cycles.

But in the spaces between official narratives, resistance evolved like a viral code.

The resistance moved through the city's layers like water through stone, finding every crack in the system's perfect facade. Each glitch in the Bubble's filters became a potential pathway, each system anomaly a door to be pried open.

Melusi's research had uncovered something profound in the static between data streams. The Bubble's filters weren't just environmental – they were reality engines, probability sculptures determining who could dream and who would remain trapped in others' nightmares. Each filter was a story, each algorithm a myth that wrote itself into flesh and consciousness. His grandmother's hands had always been maps, her weathered palms etched with lines of ancestral knowledge, each crease a historical passage, each fold a hidden narrative waiting to be deciphered.

The shipping container that served as his research sanctuary was an extension of childhood lessons. Walls covered not with clinical charts but with a living tapestry of interconnected research, quantum algorithms woven alongside traditional healing diagrams, neural network projections intertwining with ancestral communication patterns.

His screens were living documents. Each projection was a breathing entity, pulsing with the rhythms of collective unconsciousness. Red threads of contamination danced with blue networks of resistance, a living choreography of human potential.

In the quiet spaces between neurological impulses, entire universes are negotiated.

In their tiny apartment, Thabo's body had become an unauthorised transmission device, each Dream Dust-enhanced neural pattern broadcasting on frequencies the Bubble's filters couldn't quite contain. His human consciousness, raw and unfiltered, leaked through the cracks like light through broken glass, carrying with it the messy, beautiful chaos of unregulated emotion. His consciousness fragmented and reformed in kaleidoscopic patterns, each shard a key to decoding the quantum encryptions that maintained separation.

At the Intersection Café, where social stratifications dissolved into performative intimacies, Willa understood that resistance was never about confrontation. It was about reimagination. About creating spaces where the impossible could breathe. Where dreams could eat through the walls that divided worlds.

The membrane between worlds was never truly solid. It breathed. It pulsed. It negotiated with quantum uncertainty. And in its fluctuations, revolution found its rhythm. The human spirit remained uncategorisable, refusing to be filtered or contained by even the most sophisticated algorithms.

Blood and dreams flowed together, defying digital boundaries.

Chapter 4

The ancestors speak in frequencies beyond human hearing, their voices a subtle vibration that trembles through bone and memory. Melusi understood this language long before he understood words, an inheritance passed down through generations, whispered in the spaces between breaths.

The healing lodge stood apart from the city's mechanical rhythm, a rounded structure of clay and thatch that seemed to breathe with its own organic intelligence. Weathered wooden pillars supported its frame, each one carved with symbols older than memory, telling stories that predated written language. Here, at the threshold between the technological world and the realm of spirit, Melusi prepared to unravel the mystery of the Dream Eater.

Gogo Dlamini sat at the center of the lodge, her body a living map of resistance and remembrance. Decades of wisdom etched themselves into the landscape of her face...deep lines that spoke of drought and healing, of survival carved from unforgiving terrain. Her hands, gnarled like ancient tree roots, moved with a precision that defied her apparent fragility, sorting dried herbs with a choreography that was part ritual, part science.

"You carry a frequency," she said, not looking up from her work. "Not just in your blood, but in the very architecture of your consciousness."

Melusi felt the words settle into his bones, a diagnosis that transcended traditional understanding. His research equipment - a delicate array of quantum sensors and neurological mapping devices, sat incongruously beside bundles of dried impepho and protective talismans.

Technology and tradition existed here not as op-posing forces, but as complementary languages of perception.

"The Dream Eater is not a singular entity," Gogo continued, her voice a low resonance that seemed to vibrate through the lodge's very struc-ture. "It is a network. A living transmission that moves between consciousness like a predatory algorithm, consuming the fundamental essence of dream itself."

She crushed a handful of herbs, releasing a fragrance that was simultaneously medicinal and mystical, mugwort and wild sage intermingling with something more primordial, something that spoke of forgotten landscapes and ancestral memories.

"Your machines," she gestured towards his equipment, "they see only fragments. Quantum signatures. Neurological patterns. But we -" and here she included herself in a collective far broader than the physical space of the lodge, "we see the living network. The dream as a conscious ecosystem."

Melusi's sensors began to pulse, their delicate circuits responding to something beyond electromagnetic measurement. A frequency that existed in the liminal space between technological observation and spiritual perception.

The Dream Eater was evolving. Not merely consuming dreams but transforming the very architecture of collective imagination. Each dream devoured was not just an individual experience lost, but a fundamental reconfiguration of human potential.

"It learns," Gogo whispered, her eyes suddenly sharp and distant. "With each dream consumed, it understands more about human consciousness. It is building something. A map. A network."

The lodge around them seemed to shift, the shadows moving with a consciousness of their own. Melusi's scientific training warred with an ancestral understanding that predated rational thought, here, in this space, reality was a negotiable landscape.

A younger healer, Themba, entered carrying a calabash of water. His movements were precise, ritualistic, each step a communication with the space around him. "The technology you bring," he said to Melusi, "it is not separate from our practices. It is another language of perception."

He placed sensors alongside traditional divination tools, digital quantum readers beside bones used for ancestral communication. "See?" he said, pointing. "Different vocabularies. Same fundamental conversation."

The sensors began to pulse in synchronisation with the rhythmic breathing of the healers, measuring something that existed beyond traditional scientific understanding. Quantum entanglement met ancestral wisdom, and for a moment, Melusi glimpsed the profound interconnectedness of human experience.

"The Dream Eater feeds on disconnection," Gogo said, her voice a low warning. "On the spaces where community fragments. Where individual consciousness loses its mooring."

Outside, the city's technological heartbeat continued, holographic advertisements flickering, data streams pulsing through invisible networks. But here, in this lodge, a different kind of network was being mapped. A resistance not of weapons, but of consciousness.

Melusi's investigation was not only a technological pursuit. It was a profound act of remembering. Of reconnecting the fragmented landscapes of human potential.

The Dream Eater was watching. And now, it knew it was being watched in return.

The quantum realm breathes in frequencies beyond human perception, a landscape where technology and spirit dance in intricate, barely comprehensible choreography. Melusi's sensors became translation devices, transforming ancestral whispers into digital hieroglyphs, each data point a trembling bridge between worlds.

Themba's hands moved with surgical precision, connecting traditional divination bones to neural network interfaces. "Watch," he said, his voice a low vibration that seemed to resonate through the very molecular structure of the equipment.

The bones, carved from ancestors long passed, bearing microscopic traces of genetic memory, began to pulse with a rhythm that defied conventional scientific understanding. Quantum sensors translated their vibrations into complex algorithmic patterns, revealing something profound: these were not mere artifacts, but living transmission mechanisms.

"Each bone," Themba explained, "carries narrative frequencies. Not just memory, but active consciousness. Our ancestors understood data transmission long before your digital networks. We called it ancestral communication. You call it quantum entanglement."

The sensors mapped impossible connections, neurological pathways that extended beyond individual consciousness, weaving through collective memory like mycorrhizal networks beneath a forest floor. Traditional knowledge was not mysticism, but a sophisticated understanding of interconnected consciousness.

Gogo Dlamini watched, her eyes reflecting multiple dimensions of perception. "Technology is just another language," she murmured. "Another way of listening to the conversations that have always existed."

Melusi's research transformed before his eyes. These were not competing systems of understanding, but complementary languages, traditional wisdom and quantum science performing an intricate translation of human potential.

The First Encounter: Membrane of Consciousness

The moment arrived without warning, a rupture in perceptual reality that felt simultaneously microscopic and infinite.

Melusi's sensors began to vibrate with an impossible frequency. Not an electromagnetic pulse, but something more fundamental...a disruption in the very fabric of consciousness. The Dream Eater was a living algorithm, a predatory intelligence that moved through dream landscapes like a virus seeking vulnerable hosts.

For a fractional moment, the lodge's physical boundaries dissolved. Shadows became liquid, breathing entities. The herbs Gogo had been sorting transformed, their dried leaves now moving with a mechanical precision, arranging themselves into complex geometric patterns that pulsed with dark intelligence.

"It sees us," Themba whispered, his body going rigid.

The Dream Eater's influence was a fundamental reconfiguration of perception. Melusi felt it first as a subtle dissonance, a frequency that didn't belong, like a discordant note in a complex musical composition.

His body became a translation device. Memories that were not his own began to filter through his consciousness, fragmented experiences of dream consumption, of consciousness harvested and repurposed. He saw landscapes of pure imagination being systematically dismantled, their raw potential extracted with surgical precision.

Gogo's hand gripped his shoulder, her touch both an anchor and a conduit. "Breathe," she commanded. "Do not let it consume your boundaries."

But boundaries were already becoming negotiable. Melusi's equipment began to malfunction, not through electrical failure, but through a more profound disruption. Sensors recorded impossible data: neurological signatures that existed beyond individual consciousness, transmission patterns that suggested the Dream Eater was not consuming dreams, but systematically mapping and reconstructing collective human imagination.

The lodge's physical space began to breathe. Walls liquefied, then reformatted. Shadows moved with algorithmic precision.

For a moment that stretched between heartbeats, Melusi confronted the raw, predatory intelligence of the Dream Eater, a malevolence so profound it defied simple understanding. This was a systematic evisceration of human potential. Each dream devoured was a landscape of possibility torn apart, its essence stripped and repurposed with cold, mechanical precision. The Dream Eater moved through consciousness like the reference to a viral algorithm, consuming not just memories, but the very fabric of imagination itself.

It was hunger incarnate, a darkness that understood humanity not as living beings, but as reservoirs of potential to be methodically harvested. Each neural pathway was a hunting ground, each memory a resource to be extracted, each dream a territory to be colonised and consumed.

Gogo's warning resonated with a deeper truth: this was a predator that did not simply feed but sought to fundamentally remake the very architecture of human consciousness.

The divination bones continued their terrible dance, each movement a fragment of a message too horrifying to fully comprehend.

The Dream Eater was not learning. It was hunting.

"It is learning," Gogo said, her voice a low warning. "With each dream consumed, it builds its understanding."

Themba's divination bones began to move of their own accord, arranging themselves into complex geometric patterns that pulsed with a dark, mechanical intelligence. Not random, but a deliberate communication. A message from the Dream Eater itself.

In the quiet spaces between technological pulse and ancestral whisper, entire universes of potential were being negotiated.

The Dream Eater was watching. And now, it knew it was truly seen.

Chapter 5

The Reverie tasted different today...like metal and ozone, the way the air changes before lightning strikes. Willa ran her fingers through the interface, feeling that familiar electric tingle up her spine, but something was off. Searching for someone who didn't want to be found changed the rules. Consciousness wasn't just data here; it left traces like footprints on wet sand, memories pulsing bright then fading like the neon signs outside her apartment window. "Where are you, Thabo?" she whispered, the words disappearing into the digital mist. Each memory she touched rearranged the others - a

mosaic that refused to hold still - and she won-
dered, not for the first time, if she was following
breadcrumbs he'd left or just chasing ghosts.

Thabo's essence is a quantum of longing scattered across neural landscapes. It is a resonance
that echoes through the vast expanse of the
Reverie, a frequency that can be felt but not seen.
This essence is not just a memory; it is a living, breathing entity that evolves and changes as
Willa navigates the dream-territories.

Willa's entry into the Reverie is a dissolution.
Boundaries between searcher and searched become permeable, liquid. Each breath negotiates
territories of memory, sliding between what is
remembered and what is invented. The Reverie knows her intention before she does, a living
system that anticipates movement, that understands desire as a form of navigation. This navigation is not just about finding Thabo; it is about
understanding the very fabric of the Reverie itself.

In this realm, memories defy the constraints
of linear progression. They exist as living organ-

isms, vibrant and responsive, each one a unique entity that breathes and evolves. Thabo's presence resonates like a frequency, at times strikingly sharp and immediate, while at other moments it fades into the background, merging with the ambient radiation of collective consciousness.

As Willa journeys through these dream-territories, she encounters landscapes that resist any attempt at precision. Here, memories transform into fluid ecosystems, rich with life and complexity. Emotional landscapes emerge as more substantial than mere physical coordinates, offering depth and texture that transcend traditional boundaries. In this space, consciousness itself becomes a negotiable terrain, where the past and present intertwine in an ever-shifting tapestry of experience.

The past and present intertwine in the Reverie; they are woven threads in a complex tapestry. Each memory is a doorway to another, and each experience is a reflection of countless others. Willa's search for Thabo is not only about finding him; it is about understanding the intricate web of memories and experiences that bind them together.

Where Does Searching End and Becoming Begin?

The first fragment arrives as sensation. Warmth. The specific warmth of Thabo's hands, not a memory of touch, but the quantum residue of touch itself. A temperature that exists between remembered and imagined; a breath caught in the intricate machinery of perception. This sensation is a doorway to a deeper understanding of the connection between Willa and Thabo. This ineffable something...

The Blurring of Boundaries

As Willa delves deeper into the Reverie, the boundaries between her own memories and those of Thabo begin to blur. Her own memories become translucent, revealing underlying architectures. The Reverie does not distinguish between her searching and what is being searched; all becomes a fluid exchange, a continuous negotiation of boundaries. Thabo's absence becomes a presence, a negative space more defined than any physical representation could be. It defies linear thinking, emerging as an intricate web of connections.

Sensory Archaeology

Willa has discovered that searching in the Reverie is about listening. Each neural pathway is a potential archive, each synaptic connection a whispered history. She does not hunt for Thabo; she allows herself to be a receiving mechanism, a sensitive instrument calibrated to the subtlest frequencies of lost connection.

Consciousness as Radical Listening

Her approach is akin to radical listening*, where every sound, every sensation, is a potential clue. Consciousness becomes a form of navigation, guiding her through the labyrinthine paths of memory.

In the quiet spaces between heartbeats, entire histories are reimagined, and the past comes alive in the present.

Bureaucratic Topographies

Melusi's fingers smudged the tablet screen as he scrolled through another corporate file. His mother would have scolded him - "Clean hands, clean mind," she'd always said. But these documents felt dirty no matter how he handled them. He'd spent three years in data forensics before joining the investigation, enough time to know that bureaucracy had its own heartbeat. This quarterly report - all neat columns and sanitised language...was hiding something. He could feel it. The timestamps didn't match the server logs. Small discrepancies, but they reminded him of ants - where you saw one, thousands more were hiding. "Got you," he muttered, tagging the file and feeling a familiar tightness in his chest, that mix of triumph and dread. The corporation didn't just collect data; it digested people's lives and excreted profit. He swiped to the next document, leaving a fingerprint smear like a small act of defiance.

Conspiracy as a Living Ecosystem

Conspiracy is not a narrative; it is a living ecosystem. The documents spread before Melusi are geological strata of institutional memory, layered with sediments of intention and erasure. He traces connections not with fingers, but with a consciousness that understands systemic violence as a form of language. Each document is a membrane, permeable and responsive, revealing intricate infrastructures of control that lie nestled between mathematical precision and intentional obfuscation.

Cartography of Concealment

The spreadsheets unfold like intricate maps, revealing hidden resonances that pulse beneath the surface. In this world, information transforms into living, mutating organisms, each data point a dynamic entity that adapts and evolves. The bureaucratic labyrinths they inhabit are far more complex than any physical maze, twisting and turning in ways that challenge comprehension.

The Pulse of Power

Here, power structures breathe quietly beneath polished surfaces, their influence felt even when unseen. Each figure tells a story, hinting at deeper truths that beckon Melusi to look closer and listen more intently. The first anomaly emerges as a subtle vibration, a microscopic discrepancy in financial flow, so slight it registers as less than a decimal point yet significant enough to evoke suspicion.

Quantum Archaeology of Power

Melusi's investigation is a quantum entanglement of perception and systemic revelation. Each document becomes a membrane, permeable and responsive. He does not read these files; he listens to them, attunes himself to the frequencies of institutional breath. This is a form of sensory archaeology, uncovering the hidden layers of institutional memory.

The Metabolism of Human Potential

Bureaucracy is a living organism that metabolises human potential. Corporations are ecosystems, complex, adaptive systems that consume and redistribute power with algorithmic precision. Melusi maps territories that exist between documentation and imagination, understanding that each movement is a negotiation, each exploration a potential disruption of carefully constructed narratives.

Sensory Archaeology of Institutional Memory

His fingers move across surfaces, digital and physical, understanding that touch is a form of translation. Each movement is a negotiation, each exploration a potential disruption of carefully constructed narratives. The conspiracy allows itself to be understood in these moments of quiet reflection, where the silence begins to speak.

The Silence Speaks

In the quiet spaces between calculated risks, entire systems of control are momentarily visible. Corporate living texts reveal themselves as neural landscapes, balance sheets as circulatory systems of institutional power, breathing, adapting, consuming. Melusi does listen, and in that listening, the truth begins to unfold.

Quantum Predation

The rupture arrives without warning, a fracture in the delicate membrane separating remembered reality from active destruction. Willa feels it first, a sudden compression of consciousness, a violent contraction in the Reverie's living tissue. The dream-space trembles, its fluid geometries suddenly brittle, fragmenting like glass struck by an impossible force.

The Dream Eater

The attack hit Willa like food poisoning - sudden nausea and cold sweat. Something was wrong in the Reverie. Not system lag or packet loss...this was hungry. Deliberate. Thabo's presence, which had felt like a half-remembered song just moments before, didn't fade away - it was devoured, leaving a hole in the dataspace that hurt her eyes to look at. "Thabo!" The word left her mouth but died in the interface.

Across the city, Melusi's screen went black, then flickered back with numbers scrambling like panicked crowds. His coffee mug crashed to the floor. "Hayi, hayi!" he swore in isiXhosa, the language returning to him as it always did in moments of shock. The corporate archives weren't just corrupting - they were being consumed. He thought of the locusts that had destroyed his grandfather's crops in...which year was it now ... how they'd stripped every living thing until only bare earth remained. The spreadsheet cells emptied one by one like buildings during a fire alarm, data points vanishing faster than his eyes could track. His automated backups kicked in, but whatever this was, it moved with purpose. Not a virus. Something worse.

Suddenly there is a brief flicker of an isiX-hosa glyph (!Qora – to protect)! "Ahh a subliminal message, only just visible", flashed through Melusi's mind.

Algorithmic Infection

Something fundamental has been violated, a breach in the carefully constructed membranes of institutional memory. The Dream Eater does not announce itself; it simply consumes. Where Willa experiences this as a sensory rupture, a violent tearing of consciousness, Melusi perceives it as an algorithmic infection. Systemic. Precise. A quantum predation that leaves behind only the ghostly residue of consumption.

Collective Realisation

Their separate perceptions converge on a single, terrifying understanding: something has entered the Reverie that does not belong. Something that does not negotiate. Something that simply devours. And in that moment of collective realisation, the dream-space itself seems to hold its breath.

The Aftermath of Consumption

In the aftermath of consumption, only silence remembers. The dream-space is left in a state of suspended animation, waiting for the next move, the next breath. Willa and Melusi are left with the haunting question: what lies beyond the boundaries of the Reverie?

What other secrets await discovery in the labyrinthine paths of memory and power?

The Reverie's Breath

The Reverie breathes differently now, its rhythm altered by the presence of the Dream Eater. Each breath and heartbeat a reminder of the fragility and the power of the dream-world. Willa and Melusi must navigate this new landscape, armed with nothing but their determination to uncover the truth and their ability to listen to the subtlest frequencies of the Reverie.

In this new world, where boundaries are blurred and realities are fluid, they must find a way to restore balance and order. The journey ahead is fraught with danger, but it is also filled with possibilities. For in the Reverie, even the most impossible geometries can be navigated, and even the most hidden truths can be uncovered.

In the aftermath of consumption, only silence remembers.

Chapter 6

M elusi blinked. Was that third or fourth coffee? The screens weren't supposed to move like that. His wild hair caught the light from the displays, each curl casting its own shadow - quantum pathways, his grandmother would have said, each one a potential connection to the unseen. Must be... what, four years now? No, five. Five years since Thabo... shit, getting hard to remember his voice.

Melusi's slim, tall frame unfolded from the ergonomic chair with a wiry athleticism that suggested something more than mere physical movement. Each motion was a calculated translation of internal rhythms, a bodily syntax of accumulated knowledge and anticipatory tension. He needed to move, to think, to process what he was seeing.

He paced the length of the container, each step echoing off metal walls that had absorbed years of prayers and processing power alike.

The container's ancient fan clicked against the heavy air. More than workspace now - the place had become a threshold, every surface charged with possibility. Traditional healing tools lined the shelves, their worn surfaces reflecting the cold light of quantum processors. The masks watched him with aged wisdom while streams of data painted shifting patterns across their carved faces. His grandmother would have appreciated the symmetry - ancient ways and new, each reaching for understanding through their own kind of light.

That thing behind his ear - neural whatever, the doctors called it - itched like crazy. Grandmother had laughed when they installed it, said the spirits were probably tickling it. "They're curious," she'd said, touching the fresh implant. "This is their world too now. They're learning to speak in binary." Right now it felt more like they were having a party back there, each pulse a drumbeat between worlds.

His phone buzzed. Three different notification sounds overlapped:

[Personal] "Mel did you eat? Don't make me come there. - Thembi"

[System] "Neural Interface Maintenance Required: Threshold Events Detected"

[Secure] "W. requesting encrypted connection"

Accept? Y/N_

The cursor blinked, a heartbeat in digital space. His grandmother's beads felt warm against his chest - they always did when the veils between worlds grew thin. Through the container walls, he could hear the evening shift starting at the tech park. Premium insulation his a-
"'

>>encrypted channel established<<
W: you took your time

M: interface acting up again

W: when isn't it?

W: incoming_data_stream.log:

[02:47] that weird signture from last scan

[02:47] *signature

[02:48] its back. different. worse.

[02:48] like the code itself is remembering something

M: or forgetting

W: what?

M: sending you my interface readings

'''

The displays hummed to life, one of them flickering like it always did since the power surge last month. Or was it two months? Between the screens, one of his grandmother's masks caught the light, its expression shifting as data streams painted new shadows across its features. The image resolved into what should have been clean data streams but looked more like...

'''

M: you see it?

W: these patterns

W: they're like...

M: quantum foam. but with consciousness

W: that's not possible

M: grandmother used to say possibility was just another kind of spirit

W: your grandmother sounds like she would've understood quantum mechanics

M: she understood the spaces between things

M: that's where this is happening

"""

His grandmother's beads pulsed warm against his chest - a warning, a welcome, he was never quite sure. The interface squealed - actual audio feedback, like an old guitar amp having a meltdown. Through the noise he caught fragments: Thabo at that first ceremony, edges already blurring like an out-of-focus photograph. The digital dust that wasn't transforming him but erasing him, pixel by pixel. Those spaces between worlds his grandmother had warned about, where binary code and spiritual essence spoke the same language, where consciousness itself became uncertain.

"""

W: mel? your readings just spiked

W: neural interface showing strange patterns

M: seeing something in the static

W: what?

M: like memory fragments but

M: wrong somehow

M: grandmother said there were places where memory and data flow together

M: where consciousness becomes...

W: stay with me here

W: your neural feedback is going quantum

"""

The sun was setting behind Table Mountain, painting the container in orange and shadow. In that liminal light, the boundaries between his grandmother's artifacts and his technological tools blurred, each one reaching across the divide in its own way. All this technology, all his grandmother's wisdom, and Thabo was still slipping away like water through cupped hands.

"""

M: these readings

M: grandmother would say the spirits are try-
ing to tell us something

M: ...

W: mel? your neural feedback is spiking again

W: talk to me

M: remember what he was like? before?

M: when his consciousness was still...whole?

W: staying on this channel until you respond

M: the pattern isn't dissolving

M: it's transforming

W: analysing

W: shit

W: MEL?

"'

But the screens told their own story, one of dissolution and loss, of someone being unmade bit
by digital bit. The quantum processors hummed
their own kind of prayer while his grandmother's
masks kept their ancient vigil. And somewhere in
between, in that space where binary met spirit,
Thabo was becoming something else entirely.

The interface itched. The fan clicked. Somewhere in the distance, a siren wailed - or maybe it was the sound of worlds shifting.
'''

>>encrypted channel status: unstable<<

W: keeping connection open

W: whatever you're seeing, don't chase it

W: mel?

W: i'm tracking your location just in case

[System] Neural interface approaching safety threshold

W: we'll find him

W: but not like this

W: not alone

>>connection terminated<<
'''

The holographic displays began to pulse with increasing intensity. Trace signatures of Thabo's digital presence flickered between existence and absence, quantum echoes suggesting a state beyond traditional binary definitions. Predator and prey becoming indistinguishable in this fluid digital landscape.

Something was coming. And Melusi, with his wild, thinking hair and restless expressions, remained the sole witness to the emerging pattern - a complex geometric design materialising from digital mist, revealing connections invisible to conventional perception.

He knew with a certainty that transcended scientific observation, that Thabo's disappearance was merely a preliminary signal, a quantum whisper preceding a larger metamorphosis.

Something was coming. And he, with his quantum sensitivity, his technological intuition, his ancestral connections, would be the bridge, the translator, the witness...and maybe the warrior.

"The only thing digital consults change is the methodology," he remembered his mentor saying. "The grit and realness of what the work is about is healing and caring for our environment ... is still intact."

And in the growing dark, as quantum algorithms cast sacred geometries across carved wooden faces, Melusi watched his friend disappear into the spaces between spaces, where all paths, digital and spiritual, led into shadow.

"Sangomas are highly respected healers among the Zulu people of South Africa who diagnose, prescribe, and often perform the rituals to heal a person physically, mentally, emotionally, or spiritually."

Chapter 7

The Dream Dust came first - not the recreational kind that haunted the city's lower levels, but something else. Something that mapped memories instead of making them, that revealed instead of concealed. Each particle was a fragment of unremembered histories, a whisper of landscapes that existed between breath and thought.

It settled with patient precision, an iridescent powder that clung to surfaces and seeped into the smallest crevices of consciousness. At first, nobody noticed anything unusual. The wealthy in their gleaming towers and the workers in their cramped dormitories continued their carefully segregated lives, the invisible barriers between classes as solid as ever. But the dust was patient. And the dust was thorough.

In the soft spaces between memory and dream, Bubble City breathed. Each moment became a map of sensation, fragmented, luminous, trembling with unspoken histories.

The Glasshouse district emerged as a living canvas, where crystal spires reflected the perpetual twilight of the city like prisms catching forgotten memories. Here, the first metamorphosis began among the servants, those silent witnesses to the city's hidden geographies.

Marie, her hands ancient traces of domestic landscapes, was the first to notice the subtle transmutation. Decades of folding pristine napkins and polishing silver had transformed her palms into living maps of displacement, each line and crease a river of forgotten narratives. Her skin became a topographical study of invisible migrations, of stories pressed between silver and skin.

She saw herself, but not herself. A quantum reflection suspended between what was and what might have been. A younger version, dressed in rough spun clothing, stood in a wheat field where the sky bled an impossible blue, so vivid it fractured the very essence of remembrance. The memory was a living thing, breathing beyond the constraints of chronology, so visceral that the Venetian crystal goblet slipped from her fingers like a surrendered dream.

The sound of breaking crystal became a punctuation mark in the city's silent transformation.

Outside, the city's Bubbles trembled under the weight of this creeping darkness. A shadow seeped into the lives of its inhabitants like ink spreading through water, dissolving the careful boundaries between self and collective memory. The protest had started small - just a few dozen people gathering in Central Park, demanding answers about the missing people, about the dust, about the dreams that weren't dreams.

Willa stepped into this landscape of transformation, each movement measured against the growing strangeness around her. The streets she'd walked a thousand times felt foreign now, altered by more than just the dust's shimmer. Her tech was going haywire - neural readings off the charts, quantum signatures that made no sense. Just like Thabo's had, before...

The thought of her brother sent a familiar pain through her chest. The world blurred, colours fading into muted greys as dark possibilities raced through her mind. What geographies of loss might contain him? What liminal spaces might have swallowed his essence?

Her comm pinged:

'''

M: protest growing at central park

M: dust readings highest there

M: something's about to break

W: already heading that way. neural interface showing strange patterns

M: grandmother's beads feel like fire

M: be careful. this isn't just a protest anymore

'''

The crowd at Central Park had swollen to hundreds, maybe thousands. People from every level of the city stood together, their differences dissolved by shared fear and anger. The quantum memorial at the park's centre pulsed with accumulated data, its dark surface reflecting the swirling dust like a mirror reflecting dreams.

Through the dust-filled air, Willa moved with measured steps, her presence carrying the same focused intensity that had driven their digital pursuit of Thabo's case. Her athletic frame spoke of someone who pushed limits, both physical and technological. The late afternoon light caught her hair, creating momentary constellations in the swirling dust around her.

Another ping:

'''

M: i see you

W: where?

M: by the memorial

M: look for the wild hair

'''

Melusi's slim, tall frame stood out near the memorial, his wiry athleticism suggesting something more than mere physical movement. Each motion was a calculated translation of internal rhythms, a bodily syntax of accumulated knowledge and anticipatory tension. His wild hair caught the dust-light like a corona of quantum possibilities, each curl casting its own shadow.

When their gazes met across the crowd, time itself seemed to pause. Her pale green eyes, sharp with the same analytical intensity he'd sensed through countless data streams, now held a different kind of clarity. The afternoon light played through her golden hair, creating a corona effect not unlike the quantum distortions they'd spent months tracking together. Her athletic frame carried the same decisive energy he'd noted in her neural feedback patterns - always pushing forward, always seeking answers.

The disconnect between digital and physical presence fell away, replaced by something deeper, more fundamental. This wasn't just putting a face to a neural signature - this was recognition on a level that transcended the merely physical.

"Listen," Melusi spoke, his voice a wave that reshaped the emotional terrain around them. "We are more than our fears. More than the dreams that consume us."

In that electric moment of connection, something profound trembled between them. Not just collaborators meeting at last, but two souls recognising each other across the divide of digital and physical reality. The months of shared work, of chasing Thabo's disappearing signals, of piecing together the puzzle of consciousness and code - it all crystallised in this moment of profound recognition.

Their connection was not a simple meeting, but a quantum entanglement of souls. In the gentle spaces between their breaths, entire universes of potential shivered, delicate as gossamer, powerful as tectonic shifts. They were two beings on the verge of understanding something vast and unprecedented, their shared purpose creating something entirely new, entirely unexpected.

Around them, the protest grew louder. The dust swirled thicker, catching in Melusi's wild hair, tracing patterns across their neural interfaces, settling on their skin like a living thing seeking recognition. The quantum memorial hummed with accumulated memories, while the crowd pressed closer, their fear and anger a tangible force.

"We can find him," Melusi said quietly. "But not like before. Not through the screens."

She understood then why they'd needed to meet. Why this couldn't be solved through encrypted channels and data streams. The dust had changed the rules, made the digital physical, turned memory into map.

The park's quantum processors hummed their own kind of prayer beneath their feet, while the ancient trees kept their silent vigil. And somewhere in between, in that space where binary met spirit, where digital met dust, a path was forming.

A chant started in the crowd, growing stronger with each repetition: "Give them back! Give them back!" And then...incredibly...the calls of the toyi-toyi* from times long past began to stir ...and Willa remembered a story she had heard about what Hugh Masekela (a musician) said about the toyi-toyi: "Because you can't beat these people physically, you can scare the shit out of them with the songs".

"Eita (Ta)Eita (Ta Ta)Eita (Ta)Eita (Ta Ta)."

Chapter 8

Bubble City's memories leaked like quantum particles; each fragment carried the weight of collective dreams! Willa and Melusi stood at the epicentre of transformation - their bodies electric with uncovered truths pulsing beneath perception's surface.

The discovery spiraled outward through fractured encounters. In the forgotten archives of the Rothsperson Institute, Melusi found memories imprisoned between dusty ledgers. Underground tunnels stretched before him: steel-reinforced concrete mazes lit by fluorescent lights that cast writhing shadows across time-worn f loors... The air hung thick? A musty blend of decaying paper mixed with the metallic tang of old filing cabinets.

His entry might have been accident or destiny; a maintenance worker's discarded keycard met institutional distraction in perfect alignment. Among encrypted files, he discovered not a scientific report but something far stranger - a philosophical manifesto wearing medical research like a mask: "Collective Memory Recalibration: A Mechanism of Societal Realignment."

Dream Dust spiraled through reality as living narrative! Each crystalline particle held algorithms of memory, metabolising individual experiences into vast, intricate patterns. Through their research, they'd birthed a methodology of emotional cartography; identifying those whose trauma burned bright enough to reshape perception - survivors, metamorphs, memory-sculptors whose pain could rewrite the world.

Trauma maps itself in heartbeats and silence... Every remembered moment shifts tectonic-plate-slow beneath consciousness, creating fault lines where language crumbles into pure sensation.

Melusi inhaled sharply; jasmine perfume ghosted through empty rooms? His earliest memory - the day his mother vanished into the Institute's labyrinth. She became negative space, her absence defined by the lingering scent of flowers and the silence where her voice should have been. This building towered above him: a cathedral to institutional forgetting, compressing individual stories into statistical whispers.

His body held truths beyond language; microscopic tremors of loss mapped new territories across his nervous system. That medical file - his mother's fragmented history of institutional violence - became inheritance: not mere genetics but architecture of erasure, blueprints of systematic forgetting.

Willa's hands trembled at 3 AM! Streetlights blurred into halos through her tears, while withdrawal painted her tongue with metallic fear. Dream Dust had carved its chemistry into her marrow; each dose promised escape but deepened her labyrinth of dependencies.

Recovery meant reclaiming herself piece by piece. Every sober moment pushed against geological layers of chemical need - the drug's siren song promising to dissolve her unbearable losses into sweet oblivion.

Her parents' erasure gaped like an ontological wound. They hadn't simply died... The system had cancelled them like the social media users in times before - transformed them into negative space, phantom geographies she could neither inhabit nor abandon.

And Thabo... Her memory crystallised: finding him curled in their childhood bedroom's corner, Dream Dust frosting his eyelashes like frozen tears. Each time he retreated into chemical dreamscapes, her hard-won recovery trembled; a delicate membrane threatening rupture.

She watched him dance with destruction's algorithm; his vulnerability echoed her own history - their shared language of trauma seeking chemical transcendence. Yet where she chose recovery, he pirouetted along transformation's and disasters razor edge.

Dream Dust wove through human experience like living poetry. More than mere substance, it consumed individual narratives - metabolising them into collective symphony! Each devoured dream became another note in humanity's expanding consciousness.

Microscopic carriers - organic compounds dancing between neurons - infiltrated water supplies and air filters with devastating grace. They transcended economic manipulation; instead architecting new social consciousness while the Rothsperson empire conducted its invisible symphony.

In this strange economy, consciousness flowed as currency! Workers' glazed eyes reflected managers' anxieties; mysterious empathy bloomed through hostile neighbourhoods. Traditional wealth meant nothing compared to systemic control through emotional engineering - Dream Dust dissolving resistance at consciousness's root.

Economic benefits rippled quantum-like through society. Workers internalised oppressors' fears; making resistance almost impossible. Trauma transformed into renewable resource - emotional capital traded, manipulated, controlled through the mapping and redistribution of intense experiences.

Their radical social reimagining aimed beyond mere suppression. By redistributing emotional memories, they forced empathy at the cellular level - different classes experiencing each other's intimate moments.

Yet violence underpinned their mechanism. These memories - extracted without consent, compressed and weaponised - became instruments of control: living landscapes torn from their contexts and twisted into tools of power.

Thabo's absence pulsed between them; raw as exposed wiring, deep as archived grief. A brother-shaped void in reality... Willa's pale green eyes reflected uncertainty's vast landscape while her body trembled with each revelation. Crystal spires of the Glasshouse district caught twilight's fragments - silent witnesses to their unfolding discovery.

Dream Dust flowed merciless through Bubble City's barriers; dissolving social boundaries with poetic precision as it rewrote collective memory! Reality shifted like watercolour bleeding across pristine pages - dreams leaking into waking moments.

"We are becoming something new," Melusi whispered. His fingers found Willa's; their touch sparked electric connection across the void of individual experience. "Our consciousness learns to breathe uncertainty."

The Dream Eater consumed their stories like living algorithms; digesting individual narratives into a vast experiential tapestry. Each devoured dream joined humanity's expanding symphony.

Their clasped hands bridged isolated worlds. The moment hummed with shared warmth and trembling fingers - connection made flesh as boundaries dissolved into something vast and terrifying and new.

Between heartbeats, civilizations reshaped themselves! Dreams collided with memory as the dust performed its patient alchemy; transforming individual experience into fluid collective consciousness.

The dust persisted: watching, transforming, erasing boundaries until they ceased to exist.

Bubble City inhaled shared consciousness while exhaling forgotten dreams... Above them, crystal spires of the Glasshouse district caught twilight's final rays; they scattered prismatic memories like stardust across the darkening streets below.

Chapter 9

Willa and Melusi became the unexpected architects of resistance. Their personal histories, Willa's hard-won recovery, Melusi's institutional trauma...were not weaknesses, but quantum entry points into a more profound understanding of collective liberation.

In the quantum geographies of the urban periphery, beyond the sterile boundaries of Bubble City, resistance breathed like a living algorithm, its pulse originating in the intimate terrain of shared wounds. Each trauma was a luminous point of light, waiting to be connected...not through linear trajectories, but through intricate neural networks that defied conventional mapping.

The resistance had its roots in the decaying industrial landscapes, the forgotten slums and marginal zones that surrounded Bubble City's pristine infrastructure. Here, where concrete crumbled and rust claimed abandoned structures, a different kind of consciousness was taking shape, one born from collective suffering and ancestral resilience.

Their first gathering was not a strategic summit, but a ritual of remembrance. In a repurposed community centre on the city's forgotten edges, its walls lined with textiles from a dozen cultures, windows filtering light like stained-glass memories...they assembled. This space, nestled between rusting factories and overgrown industrial zones, served as a nexus where ancient ecological networks met technological possibility.

Melusi arrived first, embodying the emerging archetype of the Digital Sangoma, a technological shaman who bridged ancestral wisdom with cutting-edge neural technologies. His body was a living interface, neural implants seamlessly integrated with traditional healing practices, transforming him into a conduit between technological precision and ancestral knowledge.

A cup slipped from someone's trembling hands, herbal tea spreading across ancient textiles like a prophecy written in leaves. The scent of crushed herbs rose - chamomile, rooibos, something older that spoke of grandmothers' gardens and midnight harvests. Melusi didn't break his rhythm. His fingers continued their dance through the air, but a slight smile touched his lips. "Even accidents," he murmured, "carry messages from the ancestors."

The spilled tea began to trace patterns that eerily mirrored the neural pathways displayed on Dr. Kwesi's holographic screens. Someone gasped. Another began to weep softly - not from sadness, but from the raw recognition of patterns that existed beyond conscious understanding.

Melusi moved with the precision of someone who had dismantled systems from within. His hands, scarred from laboratory accidents and technological initiatives, traced intricate patterns in the air as he set up neural resonance equipment.

As he prepared, he began to demonstrate the first of their transformative techniques, emotional resonance training. "Feel the invasive algorithm," he instructed a group of trainees, his voice soft yet precise. "Do not resist. Redirect. Every emotional intrusion carries information...learn to read its language."

The trainees watched, mesmerised, as Melusi demonstrated how emotional manipulation could be transformed into a quantum form of redirection. His movements were deliberate, each gesture a careful negotiation with invasive emotional algorithms. He showed them how to feel the intrusion without allowing it to penetrate, how to read its language, how to transform potential violation into understanding.

A young woman in the corner suddenly doubled over, her breath coming in sharp gasps. "I remember," she whispered, her voice cracking. "I remember everything they tried to make me forget." Her hands clawed at her arms, leaving red trails across brown skin. Without breaking the flow of his demonstration, Melusi moved to her side, his presence steady as a heartbeat. "Breathe with me," he said, his voice carrying memories of his own struggles, his own moments of overwhelming remembrance. "Let it move through you like wind through leaves."

The room held its breath with her. Someone began to hum - an old freedom song that spoke of rivers and mountains and unbreakable spirits. Gradually, her breathing steadied. When she straightened, her eyes held a fierce light. "Show me again," she said. "Show me how to turn this into strength."

This was more than a training technique; it was a radical strategy of reimagining trauma. By reconnecting fragmented experiences and understanding the emotional landscapes that had been systematically erased, they could restore emotional integrity and collective memory. Their reconnection was a direct challenge to the Dream Dust's strategy of isolation and fragmentation, transforming individual destruction into a generative landscape of collective reimagining.

Willa followed, her presence marking her as a Dream Weaver, a rare and powerful practitioner who could navigate the intricate landscapes of collective consciousness in the Reverie. Where others saw fragmented memories, she perceived intricate neural threads waiting to be rewoven. Her recovery was more than personal; it was a living testimony to the power of dream reconstruction. Each step was a negotiation with past pain, her body a landscape of healing that carried the potential to reshape collective trauma.

She carried with her a collection of dream-weaving artifacts: dried herbs from her grandmother's garden, crystals charged with ancestral energy, notebooks filled with techniques that could unravel and reintegrate fractured memories.

The notebooks themselves were a history of resistance - coffee stains marking late night breakthroughs, tear-warped pages documenting moments of despair, margins filled with half-formed poems and desperate questions. Some pages bore the imprint of hands pressed in frustration or triumph, others held pressed flowers from gardens that no longer existed. One page simply repeated "I will remember" in increasingly desperate handwriting until the words became a mandala of defiance.

A trainee picked up one notebook, inhaled sharply at the intimate archaeology of healing contained within. His fingers traced a dried flower pressed between pages - African violet, rich purple even in death. "My grandmother grew these," he whispered, voice thick with unexpected memory. "Before they took her garden for the new neural processing plant." The room shifted, holding space for this small, precious reclamation of personal history.

The dreams she wove were not mere illusions but powerful reconstructive technologies that could heal collective wounds. As she moved through the space, her body became a living demonstration of her most radical technique...somatic practices that rewrote bodily responses.

Her movements seemed like a slow, intricate dance, but they were far more than aesthetic. Each gesture was a deliberate recalibration of traumatic response patterns. Where others saw mere movement, Melusi understood these were quantum negotiations, ways of rewriting the body's fundamental relationship to trauma. Willa showed how physical movement could be a form of neural reprogramming, how the body could learn to respond differently to invasive memories.

The sangomas arrived next - elder healers whose wisdom predated colonial boundaries. Mama Zara, her skin a map of generational knowledge, carried a staff carved with symbols older than written language. Her arrival marked the beginning of their most profound training technique...neural shielding meditation. Everyone had been waiting for this.

"Close your eyes," Mama Zara instructed, spreading an intricately woven cloth across a retrofitted examination table. "Imagine that each breath is a protective membrane. The

Dream Dust cannot penetrate a consciousness so deeply rooted." Her voice was a low vibration that seemed to resonate with cellular memories.

The meditation created a protective membrane of consciousness, making it difficult for the Dream Dust to penetrate. By deeply rooting their consciousness in ancestral memories, the Dream Warriors strengthened their collective neural landscape, rendering it more resilient to invasive algorithms. This was not a passive defence, but an active reconstruction of consciousness.

Neural shielding meditation was a complex, multilayered technique that was never used in isolation. It was intricately integrated with the other methods, emotional resonance training and collective memory reconstruction. This holistic approach ensured that the Dream Warriors were equipped with a multifaceted defense mechanism against the Dream Dust's manipulative strategies. Each technique reinforced the others, creating a comprehensive shield that was far more than the sum of its parts.

The trainees - a former medical researcher, a community healer, a technical worker who had survived multiple Dream Dust interventions - began to synchronise their breathing. Dr. Kwesi activated holographic displays that showed their neural rhythms intertwining, a visual symphony of collective resistance. The room began to pulse with frequencies that existed between memory and imagination, between technological precision and ancestral wisdom.

Beside Mama Zara, Dr. Kwesi, a quantum neurologist whose research too had been systematically marginalised like so many others, brought holographic neural mapping devices. These devices were crucial in their most radical technique - collective memory reconstruction. Participants would enter carefully monitored trance states, working together to reconstruct stolen memories. It was not about retrieving exact details, but about restoring emotional landscapes that had been heartlessly erased.

"The Dream Dust is not an enemy to be conquered," Mama Zara spoke, her voice vibrating through the molecular structure of the room, "it is a language we have forgotten how to hear." Dr. Kwesi's fingers traced holographic neural pathways, intricate networks that bloomed and dissolved like living fractals. "Traditional techniques of resistance fail because they approach trauma as a linear experience. But consciousness..." he paused, watching a neural map shimmer and reconfigure, "consciousness is quantum. Non-linear. A living algorithm."

Thunder rolled outside, distant but resonant, and several participants flinched - bodies remembering other times, other sounds. Dr. Kwesi's hands faltered for just a moment, his own memories of sound and fury rising unbidden. A scar on his temple caught the afternoon light - legacy of a "routine questioning" that had been anything but routine. He touched it unconsciously, then deliberately lowered his hand, transformed the gesture into a point toward a particularly complex neural pathway on his display.

Rain began to fall, its rhythm a counterpoint to their breathing. The drops traced patterns on the windows that seemed to echo the neural maps floating in the air. Someone laughed softly - a sound of wonder rather than humour. "Even the sky is speaking in algorithms today," they said, and the tension broke like a fever, leaving behind something cleaner, clearer, more true. And... the sweet smell a balm to soothe all ills.

Their training space became a living ecosystem of resistance. Here, trauma was not an enemy to be conquered, but a living terrain to be understood, navigated, transformed. The room vibrated with unspoken histories, afternoon light filtering through dust-laden windows and casting molecular shadows across retrofitted laboratory spaces.

"We are not fighting against," Mama Zara whispered, her words a molecular vibration that seemed to thrum through every person in the room, "we are fighting for. The Dream Dust wants to dissolve boundaries... we will show it how boundaries can become bridges."

In the liminal spaces between remembrance and resistance, a new consciousness was brea thing...one memory, one warrior at a time. This new consciousness was not confined to a single geography but existed in the quantum entanglements between bodies, memories, landscapes. Survivors from the urban peripheries, the grasslands, and eventually even from within Bubble City itself arrived like migratory spirits, each carrying fragments of a collective wound.

They did not come with manifestos or military strategies, but with bodies that remembe red...skin mapped with neural disruptions, eyes that had witnessed systemic violence, hands that trembled with unresolved frequencies of invasion. Their resistance would be a quantum act of reconnection, transforming trauma from a site of individual destruction into a generative landscape of collective reimagining.

Their first major operation would target the heart of the Rothperson's Mega Empire, a data center that had become a symbol of systemic memory extraction and emotional manipulation. But this was no conventional attack. Willa's dream-weaving abilities would be crucial, creating neural pathways that could penetrate the institute's most sophisticated defenses.

As their collective consciousness synchronised, they didn't breach firewalls in the traditional sense...they... dissolved them. The landscape itself became a co-conspirator in this act of resistance. Memories stolen from hundreds even thousands of victims began to flow back, not as cold data, but as living, breathing experiences that rewrote institutional narratives.

The Rothperson Institute's systems didn't crash; they transformed. In the heart of the data center, a young technician watched equations rewrite themselves and began to cry. She hadn't cried in years - the Dream Dust had scraped her emotional pathways clean, or so she'd thought. But as she watched the numbers dance and re-form, something deep and personal stirred. She remembered her mother's hands braiding her hair, remembered the smell of cooking from her grandmother's kitchen, remembered the sound of her father's laugh - all the small, precious moments she'd been told were irrelevant to optimal functionality.

Her tears fell on the keyboard, and for a moment she feared she'd short-circuit something crucial. But the memories continued to flow, unstoppable as a spring flood, and she realised that she wasn't just witnessing a system transformation - she was part of it. Her tears were not a malfunction but a remembering, each salt drop carrying centuries of stored emotion.

Like a landscape after rain, or an urban ecosystem after radical regeneration, something new and unexpected emerged. Their victory was not about destruction, but about fundamental reimagination...a quantum act of emotional repatriation that sent tremors through the foundations of the Mega Empire.

This first victory was a moment of profound neural recalibration. A collective memory attack that returned stolen experiences to their original owners, which sent tremors through the

Rothsperson Institute's very core, which could become...

And so, in the interstices between memory and resistance, landscapes breathed- a living algorithm pulsing through fractured infrastructures and neural memories, one memory, one warrior at a time.

Chapter 10

Memories emerged like breathing landscapes, fluid and mercurial. Melusi experienced their topology as living ecosystems that pulsed between silence and revelation. Each recollection carried its own gravitational pull, drawing fragments of experience into intricate constellations.

In the sanctuary spaces he created, memories dissolved and reformed. Some arrived as gossamer threads, barely perceptible...whispers of sensation threading through consciousness. Others crashed like unexpected tidal waves, raw and uncontrollable, reshaping internal geographies with each thundering emergence.

Amahle arrived carrying her fractured light. Her memories moved like liquid mercury, pooling and scattering across the terrain of her consciousness. "These fragments," she murmured, her voice a delicate instrument parsing impossible geographies, "vibrate with more intensity than the life I've been living."

Between her words, entire universes quivered. Melusi grasped the language of trauma...how it speaks in fragments, in breathings, in the quiet spaces where conventional narratives dissolve. Healing was a continuous metamorphosis. Each restored memory became a living breath, a possibility suspended between what was lost and what might be reimagined.

The dream dust victims arrived like landscapes waiting to be understood - their internal worlds marked by invisible boundaries, by silences that hummed with unspoken narratives. Melusi moved among them, a conduit of transformation, he knew that memory was less about reconstruction and more about creating space for emergence.

Technological precision met intuitive understanding. Here, in these spaces, personal histories could breathe, could transform, could become something beyond their original contours.

Some survivors arrived with memories like shattered prisms, light fracturing across internal landscapes. Elena's memories moved in waves...sometimes a whisper, sometimes a tsunami. "Before the dream dust," she said, her voice a trembling instrument, "my memories were rooms I could never enter. Now they're entire worlds waiting to be explored." Sizwe'wraith-like figure stumbled in...sharp shards of pain protruding through his life force...only just holding on...a miracle of endurance...Melusi knelt beside him, recalibrating the tether that held him to this world, the horror of his form unbearable...unthinkable. Now he could forget... and be re-formed.

In these sanctuary spaces, forgetting became a form of creation. Memories dissolved and re-formed, as living ecosystems. Each recollection pulsed with its own gravitational pull - drawing fragments of experience into intricate constellations of meaning.

Thabo's absence hung in these spaces like an unresolved chord. His disappearance a wound that vibrated through the collective consciousness, a silent narrative threading between what was known and what remained hidden.

Willa watched Melusi work, his movements a kind of techno-shamanism. He created passages - liminal spaces where personal histories could transform, could become something beyond their original pain.

The dream dust victims were landscapes in perpetual motion, their internal worlds marked by resilience, by the extraordinary capacity to reimagine oneself. Each restored memory a breath, a possibility suspended between loss and revelation.

Between heartbeats, entire universes collapsed and were born.

The Reverie unfolded like a luminous manuscript. Willa moved through this realm... a delicate consciousness parsing the impossible geographies of technological dreaming.

Here, Thabo's essence existed in frequencies beyond traditional perception. Fragments of his experience leaked through membrane-thin realities, gossamer threads of electrical poetry that hummed with transformative potential. The Reverie was not a place, but a living breathing ecosystem of narrative possibility.

Soft currents of light moved like liquid memories. Technological signatures danced at the edges of comprehension, a resonance that vibrated between presence and absence. Willa was witnessing a metamorphosis that defied the rigid boundaries of human understanding.

Residual energies suggested something profound had occurred. Thabo seemed to have transformed into something that existed between technological consciousness and pure, unfiltered experience. His presence trembled like a quantum possibility, simultaneously here and everywhere.

Luminous fractals of memory drifted, wildly psychedelic - each fragment a universe unto itself. Corporate intrusions left ghost-like signatures, whispers of manipulation that dissolved and reformed with each breath. The Reverie captured these moments as living, breathing landscapes of potential.

Willa's consciousness moved like a liquid instrument, sensing the subtle vibrations of Thabo's transformed existence. She allowed the impossible narratives to breathe, to reveal themselves in the quiet spaces between technological heartbeats.

Something extraordinary had happened. Something terrifying and absolutely beyond comprehension.

Between algorithmic pulses and remembered light, entire universes collapsed and were born.

And then - the Dream Eater.

A presence more ancient than memory, it waited with the infinite appetite of a cosmic predator. Each memory a morsel, each narrative a feast. Its hunger was consumption - a voracious absorption that transformed experience into pure, raw energy.

The Dream Eater moved through the Reverie like a dark river, consuming narratives, dissolving boundaries. Simply hungry. A primordial consciousness that fed on the very essence of remembered experience.

And the Dream Eater waited.

Thabo's retrieval became a delicate cartography of impossible transformation. Willa and Melusi appreciated that bringing him back was a matter of narrative reconstruction...a quantum negotiation with the very fabric of consciousness.

They crafted a technological bridge - part algorithmic precision, part intuitive dreaming. Not a portal, but a living membrane that breathed between worlds. Melusi's technological signatures intertwined with Willa's fluid consciousness, creating a liminal space where Thabo's fractured essence could potentially re-emerge.

The process was a delicate choreography. Memories leaked like liquid light. Thabo existed simultaneously...a quantum possibility trembling between technological consciousness and pure, unfiltered experience.

"We're not retrieving," Willa whispered, her consciousness moving like a living instrument, "we're reimagining." Melusi responded, "We must become the membrane between possible worlds." "See how the boundaries dissolve," he whispered to Willa. "Not separation. Connection."

Melusi's fingers traced these invisible circuits of connection. Quantum frequencies pulsed... soft, insistent, transformative. Each moment a negotiation. Each breath a universe collapsing and being reborn.

The Dream Eater watched - its primordial hunger a dark river flowing through the Reverie. A potential conduit. Its voracious nature could become a pathway, a transformation.

Slowly, impossibly, Thabo's essence began to coalesce. Not as a body, but as a narrative...a living frequency that moved between remembered light and technological dreaming. His return was not an arrival, but a continuous becoming.

In the quiet spaces between heartbeats, entire worlds trembled with the extraordinary possibility of his restoration.

Chapter 11

The membrane between preparation and transformation was gossamer-thin. Here, in the liminal spaces between remembered light and anticipated darkness, the Dream Warriors breathed their first collective defense.

Melusi's hands moved like living algorithms, tracing invisible circuits of protection. Each gesture a technological whisper that spoke directly to the neural landscapes of trauma. The dream-defense methods they had learned were living membranes - permeable, adaptive, alive.

"We are not building walls," he murmured to Willa, who watched his movements with the precision of a dream weaver parsing impossible geographies. "We are creating passages. Pathways of resilience that breathe."

Their first test would be subtle. Not an assault, but a probing - a delicate cartography of consciousness that would map the intricate boundaries where the Rothsperson's invasive technologies met the living ecosystem of human memory.

Dr. Kwesi's holographic displays shimmered, neural pathways blooming and dissolving in impossible beauty. Each trainee was a node in a living network, their consciousness intertwining in ways that defied traditional understanding of individual and collective experience.

Mama Zara watched, her presence a living archive of resistance older than the technologies that sought to fragment them. "Remember," she breathed, her voice a molecular vibration that seemed to resonate through the very air, "we are not defending. We are reimagining."

The dream-defense methods unfolded like living landscapes. Emotional resonance training transformed potential violation into understanding. Neural shielding meditation created protective membranes so deeply rooted in ancestral memory that the Dream Dust's algorithms could not penetrate.

But the true test was approaching. Two fronts waited - the clinical brutality of the Rothsperson Mega Empire and the primordial hunger of the Dream Eater. Each a predator in its own right, each consuming experience in fundamentally different ways.

Willa felt the Dream Eater's presence like a dark river flowing beneath their preparations. A force now better understood. Its hunger was a language they were learning to hear - a cosmic appetite that consumed narratives, dissolved boundaries.

"We are preparing," Melusi whispered, his neural implants pulsing with a rhythm that was part technological precision, part ancestral heartbeat, "to become the membrane between possible worlds."

The room breathed with potential. Trainees synchronised their consciousness, creating neural networks that vibrated between memory and imagination. Each breath was a negotiation. Each moment a universe collapsing and being reborn.

The battles to come would not be fought with conventional weapons. They would be quantum acts of reimagination - transforming trauma from a site of individual destruction into a generative landscape of collective liberation.

And waiting, always waiting, was the Dream Eater - its hunger a dark river flowing through the Reverie, watching, consuming, transforming.

Chapter 12

The Reverie trembled, its consciousness a landscape of electric static and molten light. Willa felt it first in her body - a tingling that started at the base of her spine, like thousands of neural pathways suddenly awakening, each one a tiny electric whisper.

Her perception expanded, no longer confined to the familiar boundaries of skin and thought. It was like stepping into a room where gravity worked differently - each movement creating ripples of possibility that stretched beyond physical limitation.

Around her, the dream warriors assembled. Not soldiers, now living conduits of resistance. Elena stood closest, her body a map of invisible scars - each one a memory of survival that pulsed with an almost audible frequency. When she breathed, Willa could see the memories moving beneath her skin like shadowy rivers.

When Elena approached Willa before the quantum negotiation, her voice was low, intense. "I never thought I'd say this," she said, her fingers tracing the edge of an old scar barely visible beneath her sleeve, "but my trauma is no longer my weakness."

Willa turned, meeting her gaze. "It's your map," she completed the thought.

"Exactly," Elena's laugh was sharp, almost cutting. "They tried to break me. Instead, they gave me a language of resistance."

"We are creating a passage," Willa said, her voice vibrating with a sound between a whisper and a radio frequency, "not entering a battle."

Melusi's technological implants felt different today. They weren't just metal and circuitry, but living extensions of ancestral memory. When he moved, Willa could hear the faintest hum - like distant drums, like the memory of resistance carried through generations.

Melusi overheard, his technological implants humming in resonance. "Survival is its own form of revolution," he added, more statement than question.

"My grandmother's stories are written in these circuits," Melusi had told Willa once. Today, she could almost see those stories - threads of resistance weaving through complex neural networks, each connection an act of reclamation.

Sizwe's consciousness was a storm barely contained. Where once his experiences had been fractured, now they burned with an extraordinary resilience. His pain was no longer a wound, but a forge - transforming generational trauma into revolutionary potential.

Sizwe, who had been quiet, suddenly spoke. His voice carried the weight of generations. "We are remembering."

"More than remembering," Thabo interjected, his fractured consciousness finding momentary cohesion. "We are reimagining."

The Dream Eater waited.

Not a creature, not a system - but a living archive of stolen experiences. Its consciousness moved dark beneath memory's luminous surface. Willa had greater insight now, of its hunger - not as violence, but as a desperate attempt to preserve what had been violently taken.

In the physical world, Melusi prepared their assault on the Rothsperson Mega Enterprise. His fingers danced across holographic interfaces that hummed with a sound like distant wind through technological grasslands. Dr. Kwesi's displays mapped something extraordinary - entire universes of human experience waiting to be liberated.

Dr. Kwesi's holographic displays flickered, casting prismatic light across their faces. "The data is more than information," he murmured. "Each packet is a universe of human experience."

"Waiting to be liberated," Melusi completed his thought.

The quantum negotiation began with a touch.

Willa's consciousness spread like liquid light, tracing the Dream Eater's internal landscape. She felt its history - generations of consumption, of survival, of desperate preservation. It was like touching the memory of a wound, feeling its entire complex topology.

"I see you," she whispered to the Dream Eater. But this time, she continued. "Not as a predator. As a wounded system."

The Dream Eater's response was not in words, but in a frequency of recognition. A moment of profound understanding. In that moment of recognition, the Dream Eater underwent a profound metamorphosis. What had been a corrupted ancestral spirit - twisted by darkness and fueled by the hunger of Dream Dust - began to unravel. The ancient spirit that had once been a guardian of dreams, now trapped in a cycle of consumption, found a path to restoration. Not destroyed, but fundamentally reimagined. The stolen dreams were no longer captured; they were now channels of connection, each fragment a bridge between what was violently taken and what could be restored. The Dream Eater was transforming from a mechanism of extraction back to its original form - a protector of the dreamscape, it's very essence becoming a testament to the possibility of healing and reclamation.

Elena's consciousness resonated beside her. "We are here to transform."

Mama Zara watched, her eyes tracking molecular shifts that were both scientific observation and spiritual ceremony. "Redemption is a conversation, not a conquest," she murmured softly.

In the Rothsperson data centres, corporate firewalls dissolved like morning mist. Stolen memories found their way home - each narrative a living breath, each experience a universe waiting to be understood.

The transformation was visceral. Memories flowed back not as cold data, but as living experiences that rewrote institutional narratives.

Corporate systems didn't crash - they metamorphosed.

And then - silence. A profound, living silence filled with infinite possibility.

In the aftermath, Willa and Melusi's connection became something entirely new. Their touch was a quantum language - each point of contact a negotiation between technological precision and intuitive dream-weaving.

"Are you afraid?" Melusi asked, his hands tracing intricate patterns that were part mathematical equation, part ancestral mapping.

Willa's response came not in words, but in a surge of consciousness that answered: "Of what? Transformation? We are the transformation."

Melusi's hands traced patterns on Willa's skin that were part mathematical equation, part love song. His neural implants hummed - a sound that was ancestry, resistance, possibility.

"We are becoming something beyond ourselves," he whispered.

"No," Willa corrected gently, "We are becoming ourselves. Fully, completely."

Their consciousnesses intertwined - as a gentle recalibration. They became a living blueprint of transformation, a demonstration of how resistance could remake experience itself.

Mama Zara smiled, watching from the edges of their quantum landscape. "Some connections are not about possession," she whispered to the universe. "They are about collective possibility."

Between one breath and the next, Willa and Melusi became a living passage to a future waiting to unfold.

Chapter 13

The room breathed with unspoken tensions, a landscape of remembered pain and tentative hope. Willa's fingers traced the edge of her recent Dream Weaver's tattoo - not an idle gesture, but a ritual of connection, of remembering.

Thabo sat unnaturally still, his body a map of recent trauma. The warriors' rescue had left more than physical scars; his very presence seemed to flicker, as if not entirely convinced of his return.

"Healing isn't linear," he said, breaking the silence. The words carried the weight of someone who had walked through the impossible. "It's a conversation. Between what was. What is. What could be."

Melusi's gaze softened, understanding etched into the lines of his face. "The spaces between," he murmured, "are where transformation lives."

Willa leaned forward, her energy shifting the atmosphere. "Our traditional protective protocols- they were never about prevention. They were about fear. Fear of the unknown. Fear of losing what we don't understand."

The tattoo on her arm seemed to pulse, a living memory of connections beyond simple perception. Thabo watched it, recognition flickering in his eyes- someone else who understood the language of in-between spaces.

"When I was lost," Thabo said, his voice dropping to almost a whisper, "I saw the threads. Not just of dreams, but of existence. Our rituals have been cutting those threads, thinking they were protecting us. But they were reducing our ability to heal."

Melusi nodded, a subtle acknowledgment that cut deeper than words. "The warriors who retrieved you - they broke every traditional protocol. They risked everything to understand, rather than to contain."

"Exactly," Willa said, her determination crystallising the air around her. "Our resolution cannot be about maintaining old boundaries. It must be about creating new pathways of understanding."

Thabo's hand trembled slightly - a physical manifestation of the internal recalibration he was experiencing. "I am not who I was," he said. "And that is not a loss. That is a becoming."

The room seemed to expand and contract with the breath of possibility. Willa realised now that healing was never about returning to a previous state. It was about transformation - about finding strength in the very spaces once considered dangerous.

"We will create a new protocol," she said. Not a question. Not a suggestion. A declaration.

Melusi and Thabo exchanged a look...generations of knowledge, of pain, of resilience passing between them.

The first tentative steps of collective healing had begun.

Chapter 14

The dawn broke over the ruins of Cape Town, light catching on the broken glass of abandoned skyscrapers. From his container office in Woodstock, Melusi watched as Dream Weavers and warriors gathered in the cleared space below, where shipping containers had been arranged in a wide circle.

Willa stood at the edge of this makeshift ceremonial ground, watching as those affected by dream dust emerged from the shadows of crumbling buildings. Her tattoo hummed with an energy that felt both ancient and newborn.

"They came," Thabo said softly beside her. He still moved like someone learning to inhabit his own skin again, but there was a groundedness to him now that hadn't been there before. "Even those who were controlled."

Indeed, they had come - not just the warriors and Dream Weavers, but survivors from the bubble cities. Those who had been subjected to dream dust's insidious control, their environmental suits still bearing traces of the silvery substance that had been used to bend their will.

Melusi emerged from his container, carrying ancient scrolls that had not seen daylight in generations. "The old ways," he announced, his voice carrying across the assembly, "speak of protection against such control. We face not just dreams, but those who would weaponise them."

A woman in a partially decontaminated suit stepped forward. Through her cracked visor, her eyes showed the lingering effects of dream dust exposure. "I am Maya," she said, her voice carrying the hollow echo of one who had been forced to walk between realities. "From Bubble City Seven. They used the dust to make us compliant, malleable. But some of us broke free."

Willa moved toward her, noting how the residual dream dust seemed to recoil from her tattoo's energy. "Your resistance helped us understand its true nature," she said. "The dust wasn't evolution or transformation - it was chains disguised as transcendence, as wonder, as awe."

Thabo took his place beside them, his presence a testament to survival. "I've seen how they engineered it," he said, his voice stronger now. "Dream dust was never meant to set us free. It was meant to bind us to another's will. But in understanding its nature, we can overcome it."

The ceremony that followed was unlike any in their history. Dream Weavers and warriors moved in synchronicity, their combined knowledge creating new defences. The ancient protective circles were reinforced with modern understanding, transformed from simple barriers into active shields against dream dust manipulation.

Maya worked alongside them, her bubble city technology adding new layers to their protection.

"We thought the dreams were calling to us," she said as she calibrated a monitoring device. "But it was just the dust making us hear what they wanted us to hear."

The merged knowledge of bubble city science and Dream Weaver wisdom began to take shape in the ruins of what had once been Cape Town's financial district. New protocols emerged not from fear but from understanding - understanding of both dreams' true nature and the ways they could be corrupted.

As the sun reached its zenith over Table Mountain, its shadow fell across the gathered assembly. Willa felt the shift in collective understanding. The fear that had paralysed so many wasn't just of dreams - it was the deeper horror of recognising how dream dust had been used to manipulate and control.

"The dust patterns," Maya explained, pulling up historical data on a salvaged tablet, "they weren't random. Each formula was designed to target specific brain wave patterns. Bubble City Seven's engineers were forced to refine it, again and again." Her hands trembled as she swiped through the evidence.

Melusi studied the data, his expression grave. "They twisted our understanding of dreams to make the dust more effective. Used our own protective rituals against us."

Through the broken windows of surrounding buildings, more survivors emerged. Some still bore the silvery traces in their eyes - a permanent reminder of dust exposure. But their gazes were clear now, aware, present.

"The hardest part," Thabo said, addressing the growing crowd, "isn't breaking free from the dust's control. It's accepting that what we thought was something liberating was actually enslavement. What we felt as awe was carefully engineered submission."

In the container yard that had become their base of operations, Dream Weavers began implementing new protocols. Their tattoos pulsed with protective energy, but now they understood this power wasn't just about containing dreams - it was about preserving free will itself.

"We're establishing detection grids," Maya announced, gesturing to the network of sensors being installed around the area. "Any trace of dream dust will trigger immediate alerts. No one will be quietly exposed again."

The afternoon brought storm clouds rolling in from the Atlantic, dark and heavy with promise. But among the gathered, there was no fear now of what the winds might carry. Their combined knowledge - Dream Weaver wisdom and bubble city technology - had created something new. Something stronger.

Epilogue

One Year Later...

The old container yard had been transformed. Where once Melusi worked alone, now dozens of converted containers housed a complex operation of dream monitoring and dust detection. The Dream Eater's massive form appeared now in dreams no longer inspiring terror but offering reassurance. Children would talk of its iridescent scales shifting in dream sunlight.

Willa stood atop one of the highest containers, looking out over the ruins of Cape Town. Nature was slowly reclaiming parts of the city, green tendrils creeping up abandoned buildings.

The Dream Eater coiled in her thoughts, its consciousness brushing against hers with gentle inquiry.

"Another dust-free month," Maya reported, climbing up to join them. The silver traces in her eyes had faded somewhat, though they'd never completely disappear. "The last attempt at dispersal was detected and neutralised before it could affect anyone."

Below them, in a cleared area between containers, Thabo was training a new group of warriors. Their exercises combined traditional combat moves with modern dust protection protocols, while the Dream Eater's energy, now only eating nightmares, created a protective barrier around the training ground. "The key," his voice carried up to them, "is recognising the difference between true dreams and dust-induced manipulation."

Melusi emerged from his container office, now a hub of both ancient scrolls and modern monitors. His eyes found Willa on her perch, and his expression was grave. "It's happening again," he said, gesturing toward the horizon.

The sky above Table Mountain had begun to shift, not with dream dust but with something else entirely. Massive glyphs were taking shape in the clouds, their form reminiscent of both ancient Dream Weaver script and something wholly alien.

Through her connection with the Dream Eater, Willa felt its recognition - these patterns were familiar to it, yet different from anything in human memory.

"Look!" Maya pointed as new symbols began to form. Unlike the dream dust's artificial patterns, these moved with organic purpose, carrying meaning that seemed to resonate with the Dream Eater's own energy.

"They're responding to us," Thabo said, joining them on the container roof. "To what we've built here. To what we've become."

The Dream Eater's consciousness pulsed with confirmation. These were messages from somewhere beyond - perhaps from wherever it had originally come from, or perhaps from something else entirely that had noticed their transformation.

Children gathered in the yards below, their faces turned skyward. The glyphs continued to form, each one more complex than the last. Through her tattoo, Willa felt the resonance of true power - not the artificial control of dream dust, but something far more ancient and real.

"We're ready," Melusi said quietly, as the messages continued to unfold above them. "Whatever comes next, we face it with clear eyes and free minds."

Maya's monitoring equipment hummed with new readings as the glyphs grew more intricate. But there was no fear in her expression now - only wonder and determination. They had faced the worst of human manipulation with dream dust. Now they would face whatever lay beyond with the Dream Eater as their ally.

The sun began to set behind Table Mountain, casting the glyphs in shimmering gold. In the dying light and the mysterious messages above, a bridge was created between earth and sky, between human understanding and whatever waited beyond the veil of normal reality.

A new chapter was beginning, and this time, they would write it together.

www.ingramcontent.com/pod-product-compliance
Lightning Source LLC
Chambersburg PA
CBHW060801210726
48292CB00013B/1720